HORRID HENRY'S
Sports Day

HORRiD HENRY'S
Sports Day

Francesca Simon
Illustrated by Tony Ross

Orion
Children's Books

Horrid Henry's Sports Day originally appeared in
Horrid Henry Gets Rich Quick first published in
Great Britain in 2002 by Orion Children's Books
This edition first published in Great Britain in 2012
by Orion Children's Books
a division of the Orion Publishing Group Ltd
Orion House
5 Upper Saint Martin's Lane
London WC2H 9EA
An Hachette UK Company

1 3 5 7 9 10 8 6 4 2

The Orion Publishing Group's policy is to use papers that
are natural, renewable and recyclable products and made
from wood grown in sustainable forests. The logging and
manufacturing processes are expected to conform to the
environmental regulations of the country of origin.

A catalogue record for this book is available from the British Library.

Printed and bound in China.

www.orionbooks.co.uk
www.horridhenry.co.uk

For Max and Zoë Cutner,
always first past the post.

Look out for . . .

Don't Be Horrid, Henry!
Horrid Henry's Birthday Party
Horrid Henry's Holiday
Horrid Henry's Underpants
Horrid Henry Gets Rich Quick
Horrid Henry and the Football Fiend
Horrid Henry's Nits
Horrid Henry and Moody Margaret
Horrid Henry's Thank You Letter
Horrid Henry Reads A Book
Horrid Henry's Car Journey
Moody Margaret's School
Horrid Henry Tricks and Treats
Horrid Henry's Christmas Play
Horrid Henry's Rainy Day
Horrid Henry's Author Visit
Horrid Henry Meets the Queen

There are many more **Horrid Henry** books
available. For a complete list visit
www.horridhenry.co.uk

or

www.orionbooks.co.uk

Contents

Chapter 1   11

Chapter 2   19

Chapter 3   25

Chapter 4   33

Chapter 5   43

Chapter 6   53

Chapter 7   65

Chapter 1

"We all want Sports Day to be a great success tomorrow," announced Miss Battle-Axe. "I am here to make sure that *no one*" – she glared at Horrid Henry – "spoils it."

Horrid Henry glared back.
Horrid Henry hated Sports Day.
Last year he hadn't won a
single event.

He'd dropped his egg in the
egg-and-spoon race,

tripped over Rude Ralph in the
three-legged race,

and collided with Sour Susan
in the sack race.

Henry's team had even lost
the tug-of-war.

Most sickening of all, Perfect Peter had won both his races.

If only the school had a sensible day, like TV-watching day, or chocolate-eating day, or who could guzzle the most crisps day, Horrid Henry would be sure to win every prize.

But no. *He* had to leap and dash
about getting hot and bothered in
front of stupid parents.

When he became king he'd make
teachers run all the races then
behead the winners. King Henry
the Horrible grinned happily.

"Pay attention, Henry!" barked Miss
Battle-Axe. "What did I just say?"

Henry had no idea.
"Sports Day is cancelled?"
he suggested hopefully.

Miss Battle-Axe fixed him with her steely eyes. "I said no one is to bring any sweets tomorrow. You'll all be given a delicious, refreshing piece of orange."

Henry slumped in his chair, scowling. All he could do was hope for rain.

Chapter 2

Sports Day dawned bright and sunny.

Rats, thought Henry.
He could, of course, pretend to
be sick. But he'd tried that last year
and Mum hadn't been fooled.

The year before that he'd complained he'd hurt his leg. Unfortunately Dad then caught him dancing on the table.

It was no use. He'd just have to take part. If only he could win a race!

Perfect Peter bounced into his room.
"Sports Day today!" beamed Peter.
"And *I'm* responsible for bringing
the hard-boiled eggs for the egg-and-
spoon race. Isn't it exciting!"

"NO!" screeched Henry.
"Get out of here!"

"But I only…" began Peter.

Henry leapt at him, roaring. He was
a cowboy lassoing a runaway steer.
"Eeeaaargh!" squealed Peter.

"Stop being horrid, Henry!"
shouted Dad.
"Or no pocket money this week!"
Henry let Peter go.

"It's so unfair," he muttered, picking up his clothes from the floor and putting them on.
Why did he never win?

Chapter 3

Henry reached under his bed and filled his pockets from the secret sweet tin he kept there.

Horrid Henry was a master at eating sweets in school without being detected. At least he could scoff something good while the others were stuck eating dried-up old orange pieces.

Then he stomped downstairs.

Perfect Peter was busy packing
hard-boiled eggs into a carton.
Horrid Henry sat down scowling
and gobbled his breakfast.

"Good luck, boys," said Mum.
"I'll be there to cheer for you."

"Humph," growled Henry.

"Thanks, Mum," said Peter.
"I expect I'll win my egg-and-spoon
race again but of course it doesn't
matter if I don't. It's how you play
that counts."

"Shut up, Peter!" snarled Henry.

Egg-and-spoon!

Egg-and-spoon!

If Henry heard that disgusting phrase
once more he would start frothing
at the mouth.

"Mum! Henry told me to shut up," wailed Peter, "and he attacked me this morning."

"Stop being horrid, Henry," said Mum. "Peter, come with me and we'll comb your hair. I want you to look your best when you win that trophy again."

Henry's blood boiled. He felt like snatching those eggs and hurling them against the wall.

Then Henry had a wonderful, spectacular idea. It was so wonderful that... Henry heard Mum coming back down the stairs. There was no time to lose crowing about his brilliance.

Horrid Henry ran to the fridge, grabbed another egg carton and swapped it for the box of hard-boiled ones on the counter.

"Don't forget your eggs, Peter," said Mum. She handed the carton to Peter, who tucked it safely in his school bag.

Tee hee, thought Horrid Henry.

Chapter 4

Henry's class lined up on the
playing fields.

Flash!

A small figure wearing gleaming
white trainers zipped by.
It was Aerobic Al, the fastest boy
in Henry's class.

"Gotta run, gotta run, gotta run,"
he chanted, gliding into place beside
Henry. "I will, of course, win every
event," he announced.
"I've been training all year.
My dad's got a special place all ready
for my trophies."

"Who wants to race anyway?"
sneered Horrid Henry, sneaking
a yummy gummy fuzzball into
his mouth.

"Now, teams for the three-legged race," barked Miss Battle-Axe into her megaphone. "This is a race showing how well you co-operate and use teamwork with your partner.

Ralph will race with William,

Josh will race with Clare,

Henry…" She glanced at her list. "You will race with Margaret."

"NO!"
screamed Horrid Henry.

"NO!"
screamed Moody Margaret.

"Yes," said Miss Battle-Axe.

"But I want to be with Susan,"
said Margaret.

"No fussing," said Miss Battle-Axe. "Bert, where's your partner?"

"I dunno," said Beefy Bert.

Henry and Margaret stood as far
apart as possible while their legs
were tied together.

"You'd better do as I say, Henry,"
hissed Margaret.
"*I'll* decide how we race."

"*I* will, you mean," hissed Henry.

"Ready ... steady ...GO!"
Miss Battle-Axe blew her whistle.
They were off!

Chapter 5

Henry moved to the left,
Margaret moved to the right.

"This way, Henry!" shouted
Margaret. She tried to drag him.

"No, this way!" shouted Henry.
He tried to drag her.

They lurched wildly, left and right,
then toppled over.

CRASH!

Aerobic Al and Lazy Linda
tripped over the screaming Henry
and Margaret.

SMASH!

Rude Ralph and Weepy William
fell over Al and Linda.

BUMP!

Dizzy Dave and Beefy Bert collided
with Ralph and William.

"Waaa!"
wailed Weepy William.

"It's all your fault, Margaret!" shouted Henry, pulling her hair.

"No, yours," shouted Margaret, pulling his harder.

Miss Battle-Axe blew her whistle frantically.

"Stop! Stop!" she ordered. "Henry! Margaret! What an example to set for the younger ones. Any more nonsense like that and you'll be severely punished.

Everyone, get ready for the egg-and-spoon race!"

This was it!
The moment Henry had been waiting for.

The children lined up in their teams.
Moody Margaret, Sour Susan and
Anxious Andrew were going first
in Henry's class.

Henry glanced at Peter.
Yes, there he was, smiling proudly,
next to Goody-Goody Gordon,
Spotless Sam, and Tidy Ted.
The eggs lay still on their spoons.

Horrid Henry held his breath.

"Ready ... steady ... GO!"
shouted Miss Battle-Axe.

They were off!

Chapter 6

"Go, Peter, go!" shouted Mum.

Peter walked faster
and faster and faster.

He was in the lead.
He was pulling away from the field.

Then ...

wobble . . .

wobble . . .

SPLAT!

"Aaaaagh!" yelped Peter.

Moody Margaret's egg wobbled.

SPLAT!

Then Susan's.

SPLAT!

Then everybody's.

SPLAT!

SPLAT!

SPLAT!

"I've got egg on my shoes!"
wailed Margaret.

"I've ruined my new dress!"
shrieked Susan.

"I've got egg all over me!"
squealed Tidy Ted.

"Help!" squeaked Perfect Peter.
Egg dripped down his trousers.

Parents surged forward,
screaming and waving
handkerchiefs and towels.

Rude Ralph and Horrid Henry
shrieked with laughter.

Miss Battle-Axe blew her whistle. "Who brought the eggs?" asked Miss Battle-Axe. Her voice was like ice.

"I did," said Perfect Peter. "But I brought hard-boiled ones."

"OUT!" shouted Miss Battle-Axe.
"Out of the games!"

"But … but …" gasped
Perfect Peter.

"No buts, out!" she glared.
"Go straight to the Head."

Perfect Peter burst into tears
and crept away.

Horrid Henry could hardly contain himself. This was the best Sports Day he'd ever been to.

"The rest of you stop laughing at once. Parents, get back to your seats! Time for the next race!" ordered Miss Battle-Axe.

Chapter 7

All things considered, thought
Horrid Henry, lining up with
his class, it hadn't been too
terrible a day.

He'd loved the egg-and-spoon race,
of course. And he'd had fun pulling
the other team into a muddy puddle
in the tug-of-war, knocking over
the obstacles in the obstacle race,
and crashing into Aerobic Al in
the sack race.

But, oh, to actually win something!

There was just one race left before Sports Day was over. The cross-country run. The event Henry hated more than any other. One long, sweaty, exhausting lap round the whole field.

Henry heaved his heavy bones to the
starting line. His final chance to win
… yet he knew there was no hope.
If he beat Weepy William
he'd be doing well.

Suddenly Henry had a wonderful,
spectacular idea. Why had he never
thought of this before?
Truly, he was a genius.

Wasn't there some ancient Greek who'd won a race by throwing down golden apples which his rival kept stopping to pick up?

Couldn't he, Henry, learn something from those old Greeks?

"Ready …steady … GO!"
shrieked Miss Battle-Axe.

Off they dashed.

"Go, Al, go!" yelled his father.

"Do your best, Henry," said Mum.

Horrid Henry reached into his
pocket and hurled some sweets.
They thudded to the ground
in front of the runners.

"Look, sweets!" shouted Henry.

Al checked behind him.
He was well in the lead. He paused
and scooped up one sweet, and then
another. He glanced behind again,
then started unwrapping the yummy
gummy fuzzball.

"Sweets!" yelped Greedy Graham.
He stopped to pick up as many
as he could find then stuffed them
in his mouth.
"Yummy!" screamed Graham.

"Sweets! Where?" chanted the others. Then they stopped to look.

"Over there!" yelled Henry, throwing another handful.

The racers paused to pounce on the treats.

While the others munched and crunched, Henry made a frantic dash for the lead.

He was out in front!

Henry's legs moved as they had never moved before, pounding round the field. And there was the finishing line!

 THUD!

THUD!

THUD!

Henry glanced back.
Oh no! Aerobic Al was catching up!

Henry felt in his pocket. He had one
giant gob-stopper left. He looked
round, panting.

"Go home and take a nap, Henry!"
shouted Al, sticking out his tongue
as he raced past.

Henry threw down the gob-stopper
in front of Al. Aerobic Al hesitated,
then skidded to a halt and picked it
up. He could beat Henry any day so
why not show off a bit?

Suddenly Henry sprinted past.
Aerobic Al dashed after him.
Harder and harder, faster and faster
Henry ran. He was a bird.
He was a plane.
He flew across the finishing line.

"The winner is … Henry?"
squeaked Miss Battle-Axe.

"I've been robbed!"
screamed Aerobic Al.

"Hurray!" yelled Henry.

Wow, what a great day, thought
Horrid Henry, proudly carrying
home his trophy. Al's dad shouting
at Miss Battle-Axe. Miss Battle-Axe
and Mum shouting back.
Peter sent off in disgrace.
And he, Henry, the big winner.

"I can't think how you got those eggs muddled up," said Mum.

"Me neither," said Perfect Peter, sniffling.

"Never mind, Peter," said Henry brightly. "It's not winning, it's *how* you play that counts."

Tina

and the Tooth Fairy

GORDON SNELL

• Pictures by Peter Blodau •

THE O'BRIEN PRESS
DUBLIN

For dearest Maeve, with all my love

First published 2005 by The O'Brien Press Ltd,
12 Terenure Road East, Rathgar, Dublin 6, Ireland.
Tel: +353 1 4923333; Fax: +353 1 4922777
E-mail: books@obrien.ie
Website: www.obrien.ie
Reprinted 2006, 2012, 2015.

Copyright for text © Gordon Snell
Copyright for illustrations, layout, editing and design
© The O'Brien Press Ltd

ISBN: 978-0-86278-601-4

4   6   8   9   7   5
15   17   19   18   16

Typesetting, layout, editing, design: The O'Brien Press Ltd.
Printed and bound in Ireland by Clondalkin Digital Print.
The paper used in this book is produced using pulp from managed forests

The O'Brien Press receives assistance from

Can YOU spot the panda
hidden in the story?

Mum had baked biscuits! Yum!
She put them on a plate to cool.
'Don't touch, Tina,'
she warned.

But when Mum was gone,
Tina reached for the plate.
Just one, she thought.
Mum won't notice.

The plate slipped,
and all the biscuits
fell on the floor.

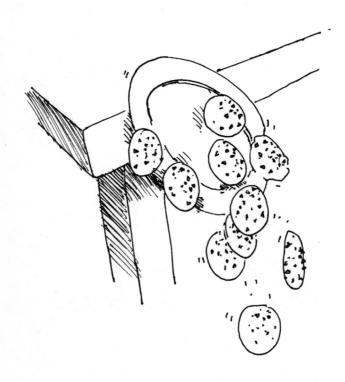

Daffy was there in a flash.
She gobbled heaps of biscuits.
'Stop it, Daffy!' Tina shouted.

But Tina munched too.

'Oh no!' said Mum.
'Tina, what a mess
you've made!
Why can't you be **good**?'

But Tina was not good.
Tina was **never** good.

She was always in trouble.

At school, she stuck the tip of
her pencil in Mary's neck.
'Hey, Mary! It's a bee!
You've been stung!'
she whispered.
Mary screamed.

Mrs Doyle glared at Tina.
'Why can't you be good, Tina?'
she said.

At playtime, she hid
behind the wall.

Then she jumped out
with a scream,
frightening all the others.

One evening at tea,
Tina took a huge bite of cake.
She felt something hard
in her mouth.
She spat out the cake.

'Tina! That's disgusting!'
said her mother.
'Oh, why can't you be good?'

'But Mum, look!' said Tina.
She picked a tooth
out of the chewed cake.
'It's my tooth!'

She held it up proudly.
'Ohh!' said her mother.
'You were right to spit it out.
And tonight you can put it
under your pillow.'

'Hurray!' said Tina.
'I'll get money from
the Tooth Fairy.'

She thought about
what she would buy:

stink bombs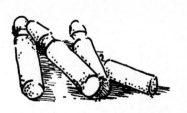

a whoopee cushion

a false moustache

a toy mouse.

Oh, she'd have
great fun.

Now, Tina didn't actually
believe in fairies.
But she didn't tell anyone that!

She put the tooth
under her pillow.

In the middle of the night
a big bump woke Tina.

'What's that? Who's there?'
she called.

Sitting on her bed was
a tiny person.
She wore a frilly dress,
and had wings on her back.
She was holding a wand
with a star on the top.

'I wish people would
leave the light on,'
said the fairy.
'How can I make
a proper landing
in the dark?'

'Sorry,' said Tina.

'What's your name?'
asked the visitor.
She spoke in a
soft, sweet voice.
She smiled a lot.
'Tina,' said Tina.
'What's yours?'

'I'm Bella. I'm a Good Fairy.'

'I don't think I believe
in fairies,' said Tina.
'Oh,' said Bella.
'I'm sorry to hear that.
But what do you think I am?'

Tina didn't know what to say.

'If you don't believe in me,'
said Bella, 'I can't change
your tooth into money.'

'I believe! I believe!' said Tina.
'You really are the Tooth Fairy?'
'Yes!' said Bella. 'Now – watch!'

She tapped Tina's pillow
with her wand and said:

**'To tell the truth
It's very funny –
Tina's tooth
Has changed to money!'**

Tina looked under her pillow.
Her tooth was not there.
Instead, there was
a shiny coin.

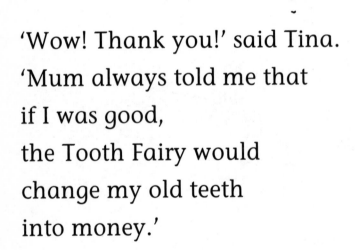

'Wow! Thank you!' said Tina.
'Mum always told me that
if I was good,
the Tooth Fairy would
change my old teeth
into money.'

'And are you good?'
asked Bella.
'Not very,' said Tina.
'Being good is boring.'

'You know,' said Bella,
'You're right. I'm always good.
I sometimes get fed up
but I can't think
of any bad things to do.'

'I can!' said Tina.

'I'm really good at being bad!

I'll show you, if you like.'

'Wing-a-ding!'
cried Bella. 'Let's go!'

'Now?' asked Tina.

'**Now**!' said Bella.

Tina jumped out of bed
and they went to
the open window.
'Ready to roll!' said Bella.
She took Tina's hand.

'**Five**

    four

        three

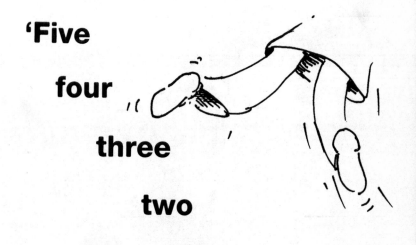

           two

              one –

                  lift-off!'

ZOOM!

Suddenly they shot
out the window.
They were flying!

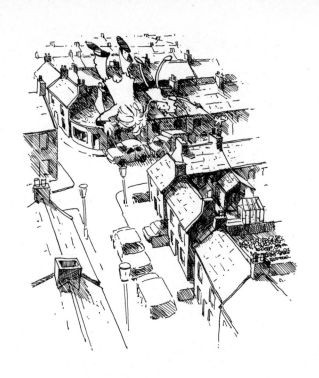

They floated above the rooftops,
and over the quiet roads
and silent gardens
that lay still in the moonlight.
'Wow!' said Tina.
'This is the best ever.'

'Well, where to?' asked Bella.

Tina looked down.

They were flying over

Tina's school.

'Down there!' said Tina.

They floated through
an open skylight
then along the corridors.
Tina pushed open the door
of her own classroom.

Now, Mrs Doyle often read
stories to her class
about Billy Beck.
He was a goody-goody boy
who was really, really good
all the time.
Mrs Doyle **loved** him.

'He never shouts,' Tina said.

'He's always polite.

He doesn't play rough games

... or pick his nose

... or eat too quickly

... or play loud music.

He's so goody-goody,
it makes you sick!'

'Just like me,' said Bella.

'Come on, Tina,

show me how to be **bad**.'

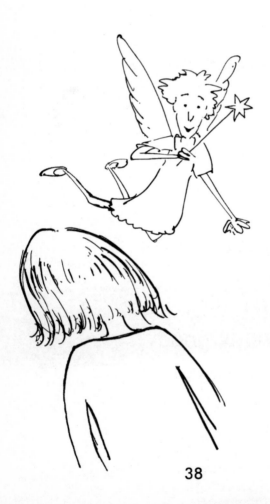

'Mrs Doyle keeps the book
in her desk. Here it is.'
Tina took the book out.

'I know what we'll do,' Bella said.
'We'll stick the pages together,
so she can't open them.'

Bella found some glue
and pasted it on the pages.
Then they slammed
the book shut.
They put it back in
the teacher's desk.

'Done!' said Tina.
'Bella, you're good
at being bad!'

'Thank you,' said Bella.
'I'm learning. How about this?'
She took a piece of chalk and
wrote on the blackboard:

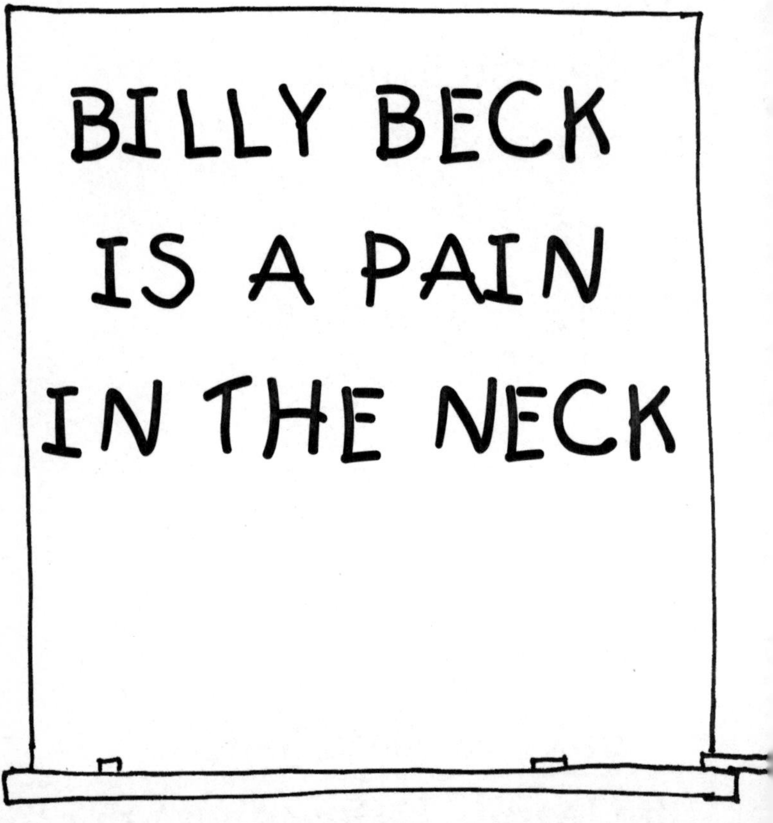
BILLY BECK
IS A PAIN
IN THE NECK

Tina laughed.
'Pretty good,' she said,
'for a beginner.'

They flew off again
and floated across
the night sky.

'Look down there!' said Tina.
'It's Mr Morton's vegetable
garden. Let's land!'
Down they went.

Mr Morton had planted
rows and rows of vegetables:
cabbages, tomatoes, onions,
carrots, lettuces, peas, beans
and marrows.

Tina told Bella that Mr Morton
was a nasty, boastful man.
His vegetables always
won prizes in the local show.
He laughed at all the
other gardeners.

There were some big marrows
lying on the ground.
They were so huge,
they looked like giant sausages.

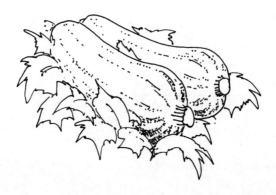

'One of his marrows always
wins First Prize,' said Tina.
'They're much bigger than
anyone else's.'

Bella jumped up on to the
biggest marrow.

'It's like a mountain,' she said.

'People say,' said Tina,
'that he uses some
special fertiliser that's really
against the rules.
That's why he always wins.'

'When is the show?'
asked Bella.
'Next week,' said Tina.

'Right!' said Bella.
'Let's get to work!'
She picked up two sticks
and gave one to Tina.

Then she stuck hers into the
giant marrow
and carved the letter **C**
into the skin.

Tina watched as she saw
the word **cheat**
appear on the marrow.

'Wow!' said Tina.
'That's **really bad**.'

'Come on, we'll do the same
to all the marrows!'
said Bella.
Soon all the marrows
had **cheat** written
across them.

'He'll never be able to put those in the show,' said Tina.
'He'll know he's been found out.'
'He deserves it,' said Bella.

'He deserves more!' said Tina.

'Watch **me**!'

She grabbed a head of lettuce
and pulled it out of the earth.
She threw it into the air.

'Whoopee!' she cried,
pulling up another.
'We'll pull up all his vegetables,
and his garden will be ruined.'

'No!' said Bella sharply. 'Stop!'
'Why?' said Tina. 'You said
he deserved it.'

'But the vegetables don't!'
said Bella. 'People can eat
all those vegetables.
We can't destroy
all the vegetables.
That would be a total waste.'

'I thought you wanted
to be **bad**!' said Tina.
'Yes,' said Bella, 'but I don't
want to **mess
everything up**.
I now know that sometimes
good is better, and it's good
to save the vegetables.'

Before Tina could answer,
a light went on in the house.
A window opened and
someone called out,
'Who's there?'

'Time to fly,' said Bella,
and Tina and the Tooth Fairy
zoomed off
into the night sky.

Back in her bed,
Tina snuggled down
under the warm covers.
She was very tired.
She held up the coin and said:
'Thank you, Bella. Will you
come and see me again?'

Bella smiled. 'When your
next tooth comes out,
I'll be here.'

'We can fly out and
have more adventures,
and be bad again,' said Tina.

'Maybe we could
be good too,' said Bella.

'We could have some bad
adventures for me,' she said,
'and some good ones for you.
Then we'll both be
good and bad –
but not **too** good
and not **too** bad.'

'Me? Good?' said Tina. 'Really?'

'I'll show you,' said Bella.
'It will be fun, I promise.'
'Okay, so,' agreed Tina.
She checked her teeth
but there wasn't any loose one.

'Goodbye!' said Bella.
'See you next time!'

She went to the window,
waved, and flew away
into the night.